This book belongs to

_____

_____

For Theo Henry John James

C.F.

For Chloe, you have always brought joy to our days and peace to our nights

D.H.

An Imprint of Sterling Publishing
387 Park Avenue South
New York, NY 10016

SANDY CREEK and the distinctive Sandy Creek logo are registered
trademarks of Barnes and Noble, Inc.

First published in Great Britain in 2010 by Gullane Children's Books

Text © 2010 by Clare Freedman
Illustrations © 2010 by Daniel Howarth

This 2011 edition published by Sandy Creek, by arrangement with Gullane Children's Books.

ISBN 978-1-4351-3007-4

Printed and bound in Guangzhou, China
Lot #:
10 9 8 7 6 5 4 3
01/13

My Special
Bedtime Bear

Claire Freedman   Daniel Howarth

Sandy Creek
NEW YORK

The sun smiled a sleepy goodbye.
Fireflies flitted through the shadowy woods.
"Time for a special little bear to be
tucked up in bed," called Mommy Bear.
"Am I a special little bear?" Little Bear asked, bouncing over.
"Very special," Mommy Bear smiled.

Mommy Bear took Little Bear's paw.
Together they headed home
through the tall swaying trees.

At Fox's Deep Den, Little Fluffy Fox
was having his bath.

"Little Fluffy Fox and his mommy are having lots of splashy fun!" laughed Little Bear. "Just like *my* bath time!"
"Yes," Mommy Bear agreed, "but your bath time is extra splashy-special to me! Do you know why?"

Little Bear thought hard, but he couldn't work out why his bath time was extra special.

A glowing light shone in Bunny Burrow as they ambled by.
Little Bouncy Bunny was listening as her daddy read her a story.

"They look happy reading together,"
said Little Bear. "Just like **our** story time."
"Yes, they do!" Mommy Bear said. "But your story
time is even more happy-special to me!"

Little Bear tried to think why . . .

In Hedgehog's Hollow, Little Huggy Hedgehog
was being tucked up in bed by his mommy.

"They look cozy!" Little Bear sighed.
"Just like when you put *me* to bed, Mommy."
"Yes!" agreed Mommy Bear. "But tucking you into bed is extra
cozy-special to me! You must have guessed why by now?"

Little Bear shook his head.

Soft breezes rustled the
leaves as Mommy Bear carried
Little Bear gently across
the starlit stream.

Half hidden in the wavy grass was Vole's Hole. Little Roly
Vole was wrapped in a cozy blanket, having his goodnight cuddle.
"That's snuggly!" cried Little Bear. "Just like my goodnight cuddles."
"Your goodnight cuddles are much more snuggly-special to me,"
smiled Mommy Bear. "Surely you know why?"

"No, I don't," said Little Bear.

Bright moonbeams silvered the path
as Little Bear and Mommy Bear
reached Bear Cave.

Mommy Bear gave Little Bear his
splashy bath in front of the fire . . .

then they happily read a story together.

"Hop into bed," said Mommy Bear
as she tucked him in all warm and cozy.
"Mommy," yawned Little Bear sleepily,
"my bedtime *is* extra-special . . . but you still
haven't told me *why*!"

Mommy Bear smiled.
"Because it's spent with . . .

YOU, *Little Bear!*
You are the extra-special part!"

"I *am* a special little bear!" smiled Little Bear
as his heavy eyes began to close.

But then he'd known that all along!